A MAN'S PLACE

A MAN'S PLACE

ANNIE ERNAUX

Translated by Tanya Leslie
Introduced by Francine Prose

Seven Stories Press
New York

Seven Stories Press
140 Watts Street
New York, NY 10013
www.sevenstories.com

Library of Congress Cataloging-in-Publication Data
Ernaux, Annie, 1940-
[Place. English]
A man's place / by Annie Ernaux ; translated by Tanya Leslie ; introduced by Francine Prose. -- A Seven Stories Press 1st paperback ed.
        p. cm.
ISBN: 978-1-64421-354-4 (pbk.)
1. Ernaux, Annie, 1940- I. Leslie, Tanya. II. Title.
PQ2665.R67P5813 2012
843 .914--dc23
[B]
                                        2012001680

College professors may order examination copies of Seven Stories Press titles for a free six-month trial period. To order, visit www.sevenstories.com/textbook, or fax on school letterhead to (212) 226-1411.

Book design by Jon Gilbert

Printed in India

9 8 7 6 5 4 3 2

INTRODUCTION

A few nights after I finished Annie Ernaux's *A Man's Place*, I dreamed that I was walking through a forest in the very early spring. Melting ice was dropping from the trees, and I felt as if I were making my way through an extremely beautiful, intense, but ultimately friendly bombardment of glittering projectiles. When I awoke, it occurred to me that the dream might have been inspired by the powerfully affecting experience of reading Ernaux's book, which was first published in French in 1983, in English in 1992, and is about to be reissued here. The clear, unadorned, often staccato sentences of her narrative—less than a hundred pages in length and divided into sections rarely longer than a page or two—struck me as having been oddly like those dazzling vestiges of winter that the trees in my dream had shed, it seemed, for my benefit, or perhaps as a message that I was only dimly capable of receiving.

   In fact, the reading experience was even more magical than the dream. Because those "icicles"—Ernaux's spare and precisely chosen phrases—had somehow managed, in falling, to arrange themselves into a highly complex and elaborate pattern. As a result of some wondrous, alchemical process, her words had come together to form a detailed and complete portrait of a human being, an animated, dimensional representation of a person, rather like a hologram. Specifically, a hologram of Ernaux's father, who, by the time we have read *A Man's Place*, seems as simultaneously familiar and unknowable as someone with whom we have been intimately acquainted for our entire lives.

Throughout the book, its subject is only referred to as "my father." The customers at the cafe he runs with his wife call him (in Tanya Leslie's stellar translation) "the boss." When his widow prepares his corpse for burial, she calls him, "my poor little man." His tombstone and the new visiting cards Ernaux's mother acquires refer to him as A— D—.

Ernaux's father dies at the beginning of the book, or, more accurately, at the start of its second section. The first passage has been a characteristically unembellished account of its author, as a student, passing the test required for her certification to teach in a secondary school. The second part opens in a way that will give the reader a sense of Ernaux's style:

"My father died exactly two months later, to the day. He was sixty-seven years old and he and my mother had been running a small business—a grocery store and a café—in a quiet area of Y—(Seine-Maritime), not far from the station. He had intended to retire the following year."

The rest of the narrative could be seen as an exploration of the distance (a half-inch of white space on the page, a chasm in real life) between the passing of the examination and the death of Ernaux's father. Of course, the two events are unrelated, or so we might think unless, after finishing the final page, we go back and reread the epigraph from Jean Genet: "Writing is the ultimate recourse for those who have betrayed." The betrayal that Ernaux appears to have in mind is that of rising from one social class to another, of moving beyond one's parents to enter a world so alien to them that their offspring might as well have taken up residence on a distant planet. Waiting for news of her first job, Ernaux thinks, "'One day I shall have to explain all this.' What I meant was to write about my father, his life and the distance which had come between us during my adolescence. Although it had something to do with class, it was different, indefinable. Like fractured love." (22)

Her book is (among other things) a drastically pared-down but nonetheless complete biography of a man who began his working life on a farm and rose to become first a soldier, then a factory laborer, and finally (together with his wife, who is the subject of an equally eloquent companion volume, *A Woman's Story*) the owner and proprietor of the modest grocery-café in the provinces of northwest France. It is a nuanced psychological portrait, composed entirely of facts and observations, of a man who worked to improve the milieu he and his family inhabited without ever ceasing to see that milieu from the perspective of the boy who had woken at dawn to milk the cows. ("He was a cheerful man . . . He had never set foot in a museum. He would pause to admire a pretty garden, a cluster of trees in blossom or a beehive, and had an eye for fleshy girls (54) . . . When the meal was over, he cleaned his knife on his overalls . . . (56) He always slept in his shirt and vest.") Meanwhile, his daughter Annie was not merely acquiring more education than her parents but gradually moving into social, economic and psychic territory from which it was possible, indeed unavoidable, to see her father's world view, his manners, his style, his language, and every small and large thing about him from a growing distance of which he too was painfully aware.

"As a child," writes Ernaux, "when I tried to express myself correctly it was like walking down a dark tunnel . . . Because the schoolmistress corrected me, I naturally wished to correct my father and tell him that expressions like 'to disremember' and 'somewhen' simply *didn't exist*. He flew into a terrible rage. On another occasion I burst out: 'How do you expect me to speak properly if you keep making mistakes?' Looking back, I realize now that anything to do with language was a source of resentment and distress, far more than the subject of money." (52)

You can't help thinking that one consequence of these troubling disagreements about language is a quality of Ernaux's writing that might best be described as *meticulousness*—meticulousness of language, meticulousness of thought. The result is a logical, rational, cool-headed narrative about the most emotional of subjects: the life and death of a parent. Early on, Ernaux reports, she attempted to write a novel with her father as its main character, a project she abandoned with "feelings of disgust."

"I realize now that a novel is out of the question. If I wish to tell the story of a life governed by necessity, I have no right to adopt an artistic approach, or attempt to produce something 'moving' or 'gripping.' I shall collate my father's words, tastes, and mannerisms, as well as the main events of his life. In short, all the external evidence of his existence, an existence which I too shared.

"No lyrical reminiscences, no triumphant displays of irony. This neutral way of writing comes to me naturally. It was the same style I used when I wrote home to tell my parents the latest news." (23)

The irony is that Ernaux could hardly have written anything more "moving" or "gripping"—or for that matter, more heartbreaking. *A Man's Place* is among the most subtle, compressed, engrossing, delicate, understated and thoughtful books ever written about family, about class, about growing up and leaving home. We feel that Ernaux has written a letter to inform us all, her readers, about the latest news: the news about what it means to be born and to die, to be a child and a parent, haunted forever by "fractured love" for those we love, and who love us, most.

—Francine Prose

AMAN'S PLACE

> May I venture an explanation:
> writing is the ultimate recourse
> for those who have betrayed
>
> JEAN GENET

The practical test for my CAPES* examination took place at a *lycée* in Lyon, located in the Croix-Rousse area. A new *lycée*, with potted in the buildings for the teaching and administrative staff, and a library fitted with a sand-coloured carpet. I waited there until they came to fetch me for my practical, which involved giving a lesson in front of an inspector and two assessors, both distinguished lecturers in French. A woman was marking papers haughtily, without a flicker of hesitation. All I had to do was sail through the following hour and I would be allowed to do the same as she did for the rest of my life. I explained twenty-five lines referenced by number taken

---

* Certificat d'Aptitute au Professorat de l'Enseignement du Second Degré, the secondary teachers' training certificate issued by the French state. After obtaining their *license*—bachelor's degree—applicants take one-year course, followed by a probationary year when they are taken on as trainee teachers—*stagiaires*.

from Balzac's novel *Le Père Goriot* to a class of sixth formers from the maths stream. Afterwards, in the headmaster's office, the inspector said to me disapprovingly: "You really had to push them, didn't you." He was sitting between the two assessors, a man and a short-sighted woman with pink shoes. And me, opposite. For fifteen minutes he showered me with criticism, praise and advice. I was barely listening; I wondered if all this meant I had passed. Suddenly, in unison, the three of them stood up, looking very serious. I too rose to my feet hurriedly. The inspector held out his hand to me. Then, looking straight at me, he said: "Congratulations, Madame." The others repeated "Congratulations" and shook hands with me. The woman smiled.

I kept thinking about this scene while I was walking to the bus stop, with anger and something resembling shame. The same evening I wrote to my parents telling them I was now a qualified teacher. My mother wrote back saying they were very happy for me.

My father died exactly two months later, to the day. He was sixty-seven years old and he and my mother had been running a small business—a grocery store and a café—in a quiet area of Y— (Seine-Maritime), not far from the station. He had intended to retire the following year. Quite often, and just for an instant, I can't recollect which came first: that windy April in Lyon when I stood waiting at the Croix-Rousse bus stop, or that stifling month of June, the month of his death.

It was a Sunday, in the early afternoon.

My mother appeared at the top of the stairs. She was dabbing her eyes with the napkin she must have taken with her when she went upstairs after lunch. She said in a blank voice: "It's all over." I have no recollection of the minutes that followed. All I remember are my father's eyes, staring at something behind me, in the far distance, and the curled lips exposing his gums. I believe I asked my mother to shut his eyes. Also standing round the bed were my mother's sister and her husband. They offered to help us wash and shave the body before it grew stiff. My mother suggested that we dress him in the suit he had bought for my wedding three years previously. There was an air of simplicity about the whole scene, no crying or shouting, just my mother's red eyes and the frozen rictus on her face. Our movements were calm and orderly, accompanied by simple words. My uncle and aunt kept saying, "He made a quick job of it," or, "Doesn't he look different." My mother spoke to my father as if he were still alive, or inhabited by a form of life apart, like a newborn baby. Several times she affectionately called him: "My poor little man."

After my father had been shaved, my uncle straightened the body and held it up so that we could remove the shirt he had been wearing for the last few days and change it for a clean one. His head hung forward on his bare chest, mottled with tiny veins. For the first time in my life I saw my father's penis. My mother covered it up quickly with the clean shirt tails, exclaiming light-heartedly: "Hide your misery, my poor man!" When the body had been washed, my father's hands were joined together around a rosary. I can't remember whether it was my aunt or my mother who said, "He looks nicer like that," meaning more decent, more presentable. I closed the shutters and woke up my son who was having an afternoon nap in the next room. "Grandpa's having a snooze."

My uncle broke the news to the family in Y——, who immediately came round. They went upstairs with my mother and myself and stood in front of the bed. After a few moments' silence, they talked in hushed voices about my father's illness and his sudden death. When they came downstairs we gave them something to drink in the café.

I don't remember the doctor who was called in to sign the death certificate. Within a few hours, my father's face had changed beyond all recognition.

Towards the end of the afternoon I happened to be in the room on my own. The sunlight filtered through the shutters on to the linoleum floor. He was no longer my father. His sunken features seemed to have developed into one large nose. In his dark blue suit, which hung loosely around his body, he looked like a bird lying on its back. The face he'd had just after his death—that of a man with wide, staring eyes—had already gone. I would never see that face again either.

We started to think about the funeral, the undertakers' firm, the service, the announcements and our mourning clothes. I felt that these preparations had nothing to do with my father. They concerned a ceremony which for some reason he would be unable to attend. My mother was extremely agitated. She told me that the night before he died, my father—who could no longer speak—had groped towards her in an attempt to kiss her. She added: "You know, he was a handsome lad in his youth."

The smell set in on the Monday. It was something I hadn't imagined. First faint, then overpowering; the stench of flowers left to rot in a vase of stagnant water.

My mother closed the business just for the funeral. Otherwise she would have lost customers and she couldn't afford to do that. The body of my dead father was lying upstairs while she served pastis and red wine downstairs. In distinguished society, grief at the loss of a loved one is expressed by tears, silence and dignity. The social conventions observed by my mother, and for that matter the rest of the neighbourhood, had nothing to do with dignity. Between my father's death on the Sunday and his burial the following Wednesday, the regulars would sit down and comment on the news laconically. They would speak in low voices, "He went out like a light," or else affect a cheerful attitude, "So the boss finally packed it in!" They told us how they felt when they had heard the news, "It knocked me for six, it did," or "I didn't know what to think." They wanted my mother to know that she was not alone in her grief. An act of courtesy on their part. Many customers recalled the last time they had seen him alive and in good health, searching their memories for all the details of that last encounter, the exact time and place, the words they had spoken and what the weather had been like that day. Such a painstaking description of a time when being alive was simply taken for granted showed what a terrible shock my father's death had been for them. They also asked to see "the boss" out of politeness. My mother didn't agree to all their requests. She distinguished between the good customers, prompted by genuine feelings of sympathy, and the bad ones, whose sole motive was curiosity. Just about all the regular customers were allowed to pay their last respects to my father. The wife of a foreman who lived nearby was turned down because he had always loathed her, her and her tight, puckered lips.

The undertakers came on the Monday. The stairway leading from the kitchen to the bedrooms turned out to be too narrow for the coffin. The body had to be wrapped in a plastic bag and dragged, rather than carried, to the coffin which lay downstairs in the middle of the café, closed for an hour. It was a laborious operation, punctuated by the men's comments on the best way to proceed, how to negotiate the corners and so on.

There was a dip in the pillow where his head had rested since Sunday. We didn't clean the room while the body was still there. My father's clothes were lying on the chair where he had left them. I unzipped the overall pocket and took out a wad of bank notes, the takings of the previous Wednesday. I threw away the medicine and put his clothes with the dirty laundry.

The day before the funeral we cooked a side of veal for the meal which was to follow the ceremony. When people do one the honour of attending a burial service, one can hardly send them home with an empty stomach. My husband arrived in the evening, suntanned, embarrassed by a bereavement in which he had no part. He seemed more out of place then than he had ever been. We slept in the only double bed, the one where my father had died.

In church there were quite a few people from our neighbour-hood, housewives and also factory hands who had taken an hour off work. Naturally, none of the other shopkeepers had made the effort, neither had the "high-ranking" officials with whom my father had dealt over the years. He didn't belong to anything or take part in anything, just paid his yearly contribution to the tradesmen's union. In his funeral oration, the priest spoke of "an honest, hard-working life" and "a man who had never done anyone any harm."

Then there were the handshakes. Owing to a mistake made by the sacristan conducting the service, everyone who had shaken hands with us came round a second time. Maybe he devised this stratagem to increase the number of mourners. The second round of handshakes took place quickly and in silence. At the graveside, when the coffin was lowered into the pit, swaying between the ropes, my mother burst into tears as she had done at my wedding during the service.

We held the funeral lunch in the café, where the tables had been set up in long rows. After a difficult start, the conversation began to flow. The child, who'd had a good sleep, went from one guest to the next, offering a flower, some pebbles or whatever he could find in the garden. My father's brother, who was sitting at the far end of the room, leaned over and shouted in my direction: "Remember when your father used to take you to school on his bike?" He had the same voice as my father. The guests left around five o'clock. We put the tables away in silence. My husband took the train home that evening.

I stayed on with my mother for a few days, to settle the usual formalities which occur after someone has died: registering the death at the town hall, paying the undertakers, replying to messages of sympathy and ordering new visiting cards, *widow of the late A— D—*. It was a blank, empty period, devoid of thought. On several occasions, as I was walking down the street, I thought, "I'm a grown-up now." (My mother used to say to me, because of my periods, "Now you're a big girl.")

We collected my father's clothes so that we could give them to people who might need them. The jacket he wore every day was hanging up in the storeroom. In it I found his wallet. There was some money, his driving licence and in the part which folds back, a photograph slipped inside a newspaper cutting. An old photograph with serrated edges. It showed a group of workers all wearing caps, arranged in three rows, staring straight at the camera. The sort of photograph one found in history books to "illustrate" an industrial strike or the *Front Populaire*. I spotted my father in the back row, looking serious, almost worried. Many were laughing. The newspaper cutting gave the results of the entrance exam to the teachers' training college in Rouen, listed in order of merit. The second name was mine.

My mother gradually calmed down. She continued to serve the customers as before. Living on her own, she developed sunken features. She took to visiting the graveyard early every morning before she opened the shop.

On the train journey home that Sunday, I tried to keep my son entertained so that he would behave himself. People travelling first-class have no taste for noise and restless children. I suddenly realized with astonishment: "Now I really am *bourgeois*" and "It's too late now."

Later that summer, while I was waiting for news of my first job, I thought to myself: "One day I shall have to explain all this." What I meant was to write about my father, his life and the distance which had come between us during my adolescence. Although it had something to do with class, it was different, indefinable. Like fractured love.

A while later I started writing a novel in which my father was the main character. Halfway through the book I began to experience feelings of disgust.

I realize now that a novel is out of the question. If I wish to tell the story of a life governed by necessity, I have no right to adopt an artistic approach, or attempt to produce something "moving" or "gripping." I shall collate my father's words, tastes and mannerisms, as well as the main events of his life. In short, all the external evidence of his existence, an existence which I too shared.

No lyrical reminiscences, no triumphant displays of irony.

This neutral way of writing comes to me naturally. It was the same style I used when I wrote home telling my parents the latest news.

His story opens in a small village near Caux, twenty-five kilometres from the coast, a few months before the turn of the century. Those who didn't have any land were *hired* by the wealthy farmers of the area. My grandfather worked as a carter on one of these farms. In summer he also helped out with the haymaking and harvesting. He had done nothing else all his life since the age of eight. On Saturday evenings he brought back the week's pay to his wife and she gave him his Sunday off so that he could go and play dominoes and have a couple of drinks. He came home drunk, feeling thoroughly depressed. At the slightest thing he would lash out at the children with his cap. He was a harsh character, nobody dared pick a quarrel with him. His wife *really had it tough*. His meanness was the driving force which helped him resist poverty and convince himself that he was a man. What really enraged him was to see one of the family reading a book or a newspaper in his house. He hadn't had time to learn how to read or write. On the other hand, he could certainly count.

I only saw my grandfather once, in the old people's home

where he was to die three months later. Holding me by the hand, my father took me through a huge ward and led me between two rows of beds up to a little old man with a fine head of white, curly hair. He was a kind-hearted soul, laughing all the time as he watched me with his twinkling eyes. My father slipped him a quarter bottle of *eau-de-vie* which he hid between the sheets.

Every time they spoke of him to me, they started by saying, "He could neither read nor write," as if this initial statement was necessary to explain his life and personality. My grandmother had learned how to read and write at convent school. Like the other women in the village, she was employed as a cottage weaver by one of the factories in Rouen. She worked in an airless room, where the faint daylight came through long, narrow apertures scarcely wider than loopholes. The material had to be protected from the sunlight. She was a clean woman, with regard to both personal hygiene and domestic matters. In our village this was seen as the greatest virtue of all: the neighbours inspected the washing on the line to see how white and worn it was, and they knew exactly whose night bucket had been emptied. Although the houses were separated by hedges and embankments, nothing escaped people's attention, not even at what time the men rolled in from the café, or which woman's sanitary towels were conspicuous by their absence.

My grandmother even had style. At parties she wore a cardboard bustle, and she didn't pee standing up and fully-dressed, like most country women did, simply because it was more convenient. As she approached her forties, having borne five children, she was given to bouts of depression and would stop talking to people for several days at a time. Later she developed rheumatism in her hands and legs. In the hope of getting better, she would visit Saint Riquier and Saint Guillaume du Désert, rubbing the statue with a cloth which she applied to her inflamed limbs. She gradually lost the use of her legs. They hired a carriage to take her to see the saints.

They lived in a small house with beaten earth floors and a thatched roof. All you needed to do before sweeping the floor was sprinkle it with water. They lived on their own poultry and garden vegetables, and the dairy produce my grandfather got from the farmer. Confirmations and wedding receptions were planned several months in advance. People went hungry for three days so as to make the most of it. On one occasion a child who was recovering from scarlet fever died choking while he vomited the pieces of chicken which had been forced upon him. On Sunday afternoons in summer they went to "village fêtes" where one danced and played games. One day my father reached the top of the greasy pole but slipped down before managing to unhook the basket of provisions. My grandfather flew into a rage which lasted for hours. "*You clumsy oaf.*"

Crossing the bread, going to mass, attending Easter communion: religion, like hygiene, gave them a sense of dignity. They dressed in their Sunday best, sang the Credo together with the wealthy landowners and put a few coins in the collection plate. My father was a choirboy and he liked to accompany the priest when he was called in to administer Holy Communion. The men took off their hats as they walked past.

The children always had worms. To get rid of them, a small pouch filled with garlic was sewn into the inside of their shirts, near their navel. In winter their ears were stuffed with cotton wool. When I read Proust or Mauriac, I cannot believe they are writing about the time when my father was a child. In his case it was more like the Middle Ages.

He had to walk two kilometres to get to school. Every Monday the teacher inspected their fingernails and the front of their vest, and checked their hair for lice. He was a harsh man and rapped the boys' fingers with an iron ruler. In short, he was *respected*. Some of his pupils were among the first in their *canton* to have passed their primary certificate; one or two even made it to teachers' training college. My father missed class when he had to harvest the apples, tie the straw and hay into sheaves, and sow and reap whatever was in season. When he and his elder brother went back to school, the master would yell: "So your parents want you to remain as ignorant as they are!" He managed to learn how to read and write properly. He liked learning. (In those days one just said learning, like eating or drinking.) He liked drawing too: heads, or sometimes animals. At the age of twelve, he was in his last year as a junior. My grandfather took him away from school and got him a job on the farm where he himself worked. One couldn't afford to go on feeding an idle person. "One didn't even think about it, it was the same for everyone."

My father's school reader was called *Le Tour de la France par Deux Enfants*. In it one could find the oddest sentences, for instance:

One should learn always to be content with one's lot (p. 186 of the 326th edition)

Charity towards the poor is the most precious thing in the world (p. 11)

A family blessed with affection possesses the greatest riches of all (p. 260)

The most gratifying thing about wealth is that it helps alleviate the poverty of others (p. 130)

Its moral recommendations for poor children were as follows:

An industrious man never wastes a single minute and at the end of the day he discovers that every hour has brought him something new. On the other hand, an idle man is always finding excuses to put off his work; he falls asleep and lets his attention wander, not only in bed but also at mealtimes and during conversation. The day draws to an end and he finds he has achieved nothing. The months and years go by, old age is suddenly upon him, and still he has achieved nothing.

It was the only book he remembered, "Somehow it seemed real to us."

He started milking the cows at five o'clock in the morning, cleaning out the stables, grooming the horses, and milking the cows again in the evening. In exchange he was given a place to sleep, free meals, some pocket money, and they did his laundry for him. He slept above the stables on a straw mattress with no sheets. All night long the horses would dream, beating against the ground with their hooves. He thought about his parents' house, which had now become forbidden territory. Every so often one of his sisters—a maid of all work—appeared at the fence with her bundle of belongings, staring silently. She could never say why she had run away from her employers yet again. The grandfather would swear at her. In the evening he took her back to her bosses' house, covering her with shame.

My father had a lively, playful personality. He loved telling stories and playing tricks on people. There was nobody his age on the farm. On Sundays he served at mass with his brother, who also worked as a cowherd. He joined in the "village fêtes," danced with the girls and met up with his old schoolmates. *We were happy in spite of everything. We had to be.*

He continued to work as a farm hand until he was called up. One didn't count the hours one worked. The farmers used to scrimp and save. One day the slice of meat served to an old cowherd stirred: underneath, it was crawling with worms. The situation had become intolerable. The old boy stood up and demanded that they no longer be treated as dogs. He was given another piece of meat. It wasn't *The Battleship Potemkin*.

From dawn until dusk, there was the October drizzle, the baskets of apples one tipped into the cider press, the chicken droppings one shovelled into buckets, and the rough working conditions which made one hot and thirsty. On the other hand, there was the *galette des rois*,* the jokes in the Vermot almanac, the home-made cider, the frogs one blew to bits with a straw, the roasted chestnuts and Shrove Tuesday, "Tipety, tipety, toe, give me a pancake and I will go." It would be easy to write something along those lines. The relentless passing of the seasons, the simple joys and quiet of the countryside. The

---

* A round, flat cake made of puff pastry and filled with almond paste, traditionally consumed on Twelfth Night and containing a lucky charm. The person who gets this charm is proclaimed king and given a gold paper crown.

land my father worked belonged to others. He saw no beauty in it, the magnificence of Mother Earth and other such myths were lost on him.

During the First World War the only people left behind on the farms were the young, like my father, and the old. They were treated with consideration. He followed the advance of the troops on a map pinned up on the kitchen wall, took to reading naughty magazines and went to the cinema in Y—. Although everyone read out loud the text below the pictures, many hadn't time to reach the end of the line. He used the slang he had picked up from his brother when he came home on leave. The washing of the housewives whose husbands had been sent to the battleground was subjected to close scrutiny by the other women in the village. Every month they made sure that none of the linen was missing.

The war revolutionized people's lives. The villagers took up the yo-yo and drank wine instead of cider when they went to the café. The girls who went dancing grew less and less keen on country boys because of the smell that clung to them.

My father discovered the world through his national service: Paris, the *métro*, a town in Lorraine, the uniform that made them all equal, companions from all over France and the military barracks, larger than a real castle. They let him exchange his own teeth—ruined by apple cider—for a new dental plate. He frequently had his photograph taken.

When he returned home, he decided to give up "culture," which was what he called the world of farming. The other meaning of the word, and its spiritual implications, held no interest for him.

Naturally, the only alternative was factory work. At the end of the war, Y— was just starting to become industrialized. My father got a job at a rope factory which took on boys and girls from the age of thirteen. He worked indoors, on dry, clean premises. There were set working hours, and separate lavatories and cloakrooms for men and women. After the siren was sounded in the evening, he was free and he no longer smelt of the dairy. He was out of the first circle. One could find better-paid jobs in Rouen and Le Havre but it meant leaving the family, the poor, forlorn mother, and braving the smart town boys. Eight years of cattle and country plains had dulled his nerve.

He was considered respectable, which for a worker meant that he wasn't lazy and didn't drink or live it up. He was keen on the cinema and the charleston but kept away from cafés. He wasn't politically minded and didn't belong to a union; his superiors approved. He had managed to buy himself a bicycle and would put aside some money every week.

My mother must have been impressed by all this when she met him at the rope factory. Before that she had worked in a margarine plant. A tall, dark man with grey eyes, he held himself upright and was a trifle conceited. "My husband never looked working-class."

She had lost her father. My grandmother was a cottage weaver who took in people's laundry and ironing to finish bringing up the last of her six children. On Sundays my mother and her sisters went to the cake shop, where they bought a paper cornet filled with pastry crumbs. At first my parents weren't allowed to go out together. My grandmother didn't want her girls to be taken away from her too soon: each time one left, it meant parting with three-quarters of her pay.

My father's sisters, who worked as housemaids for middle-class families, looked down on my mother. Factory girls were accused of not knowing how to make their beds and of running after the boys. The village people disapproved of her. She wanted to copy the fashion she read about in magazines: she wore short dresses, made up her eyes, painted her fingernails and was among the first to have her hair cut short. She had a loud, booming laugh. Despite what they said, she never let herself be touched up in the lavatories, but went to mass every Sunday and had made the effort to embroider her trousseau and hemstitch her sheets herself. She was a lively, cheeky worker. One of her favourite remarks was: "I'm just as good as them."

In her wedding photograph, one can see her knees. Under the half-veil hugging her forehead, she is staring hard at the camera. She looks like Sarah Bernhardt. My father is standing at her side, with his small moustache and starched white collar. Neither of them is smiling.

She was always ashamed of sex. They never showed their affection or gave each other caresses. In front of me he would give her a quick peck on the cheek, almost, it seemed, out of obligation. Quite often he would say ordinary things to her, staring straight into her eyes, while she lowered her gaze and tried not to smile. As I grew up I realized he was alluding to sexual matters. He liked to hum *Parlez-moi d'amour*, she gave a poignant rendering of *Voici mon corps pour vous aimer* at family gatherings.

He had learnt that the only way to escape one's parents' poverty was not to *impregnate* a woman.

They rented accommodation in Y——, in a group of houses on a busy street with a back courtyard shared by the other tenants. Two rooms on the ground floor and two on the floor above. It was the dream of the "upstairs bedroom" come true and it meant a lot to my mother. Thanks to my father's savings, they managed to get everything they needed: a set of dining-room furniture and a wardrobe with a mirror for the bedroom. A little girl was born and so my mother stayed at home. She was bored. My father left the rope factory for a better-paid job with a roofer.

Originally it had been her idea, the day they brought my father home, voiceless and badly shaken, after falling from a rafter he had been mending. Why not take over a business? They started saving again. They ate lots of bread and pork. Among the business available, they had to choose one which required a small amount of capital and no particular skills, just buying and reselling goods. It had to be inexpensive because it would bring in little money. On Sundays they would get out their bikes and go and visit small cafés and village stores. They asked around to see whether there was any competition in the neighbourhood. They were afraid of being done, afraid they would lose everything and lapse back into working-class poverty.

L—, thirty kilometres from Le Havre. The town was steeped in fog all day during the winter months, especially in the narrow part which followed the river banks, known as the Valley. It was an industrial estate built around a cotton mill, one of the most important in the area up to the fifties, once the property of the Desgenetais family and subsequently bought out by Boussac. After finishing school, the girls were taken on at the mill. Later they would leave their children at the crèche, open from six o'clock in the morning. Three-quarters of the male population were employed in the weaving industry. The only grocery in the area lay at the bottom of the Valley. The ceiling was so low one could touch it with one's hand. It had dark rooms which needed electricity in broad daylight and a tiny courtyard with a lavatory which emptied directly into the river. It wasn't that they liked the setting but, after all, they *had to live.*

They took out a loan to buy the business.

At first, it was dreamland. Whole shelves of food and drink, tinned pâté and packets of biscuits. They were surprised at earning money so easily, by expending so little energy: just ordering the goods, unpacking them, weighing them and keeping the accounts. "Thank you. Good afternoon." The first few days, as soon as the bell rang, they both rushed into the shop, firing the usual questions, "Can I get you anything else?" They enjoyed it, they were the boss and the boss's wife.

They began to have doubts when one of the customers, after filling her shopping bag, said in a low voice: "I'm a bit hard up at the moment, do you think I could pay you on Saturday." The scene was repeated with another woman, and then another. It was a matter of either giving them credit or else going back to the factory. Credit seemed to be the lesser of the two evils.

Facing up to the situation meant that luxuries were out. No aperitifs or tinned delicacies except on Sundays. It also meant falling out with the family, to whom one had given liberally at first, to show that one had the means. They were always afraid they would *eat into their capital.*

In those days, especially in winter, I would come home from school breathless, dying for something to eat. None of the lights were on in the house. They would both be in the kitchen. He would be sitting at the table, staring out of the window, she, standing by the gas cooker. I was greeted by a wall of stony silence. Occasionally he or she would say: "We'll have to sell." It wasn't even worth starting on my homework. People did their shopping *elsewhere*, at the Co-op, the Familistère or wherever. At that point any innocent customer who walked through the door seemed to be a slap in the face. He was treated like a dog and made to pay for those who never came. The world was leaving us behind.

Running a store in the Valley was barely more profitable than working in a factory. My father had to get a job on a building site in the Basse-Seine. He worked in big rubber boots because of the water. One didn't have to know how to swim. During the day my mother ran the business on her own.

He was both worker and shopkeeper and, as such, was doomed to a life of solitude and distrust. He didn't belong to a union. He was afraid of the right-wing Croix-de-Feu partisans, who marched through L—, and of the Reds, who were after his business. He kept his ideas to himself. *You don't want ideas when you're in trade.*

They gradually carved a niche for themselves over the years, hovering above the poverty line, but only just. Because they granted credit they had kept the large, working-class families, the ones who were down to their last penny. They realized that it was the needy who supported them and were understanding, seldom refusing to "chalk it up." At the same time they felt they had the right to *give a good talking to* those who turned up penniless, and to scold the child who had been sent to the shop empty-handed by his mother because it was the end of the week. "Tell your mother she'd better pay, or else I'll stop serving her." They were no longer the humiliated party.

Dressed in a white coat, she was the perfect shopkeeper. He kept on his overalls to serve. Unlike the other women, she didn't say, "My husband will have a fit if I do that, or if I go there." She constantly *battled* with him to get him to go to church—he had stopped attending mass during his national service—and to give up his *bad manners* (which meant behaving like a labourer or a worker). He left her in charge of the deliveries and the accounts. She was the sort of woman who could go everywhere, in other words, she could "fit in" socially. He admired her, although he teased her whenever she announced, "I've broken wind."

He got a job with the Standard Oil refinery, which was on the estuary of the river Seine. He did the night shift. He had trouble sleeping during the day because of the customers. His face became swollen and the smell of oil clung to his body: it was inside him and it became his only nourishment. He stopped eating. He was earning a high salary and prospects were good. The workers were promised a magnificent estate with indoor bathrooms and lavatories, and private gardens too.

In the autumn, the fog lingered in the Valley all day. During heavy rainstorms the river flooded the house. To get rid of the water voles, he bought a short-haired bitch who broke their spines with a single snap of her jaws.

"There were others worse off."

The year 1936 was to be remembered as a dream. Although he was astonished at what the new political order had achieved, he had the sad conviction that the situation wouldn't last.

The business never closed. He spent his paid holidays behind the counter. Their relatives turned up and were duly pampered. They were only too happy to display such abundant provisions to the brother-in-law, be he a railwayman or a boilermaker. Behind their backs, they were referred to as the rich, which was the worst possible insult.

He didn't drink. He wanted to *maintain his status*. To look more like a shopkeeper than a worker. In the oil refinery, he was made foreman.

It's taking me a long time to write. By choosing to expose the web of his life through a number of selected facts and details, I feel that I am gradually moving away from the figure of my father. The skeleton of the book takes over and ideas seem to develop of their own accord. If on the other hand I indulge in personal reminiscence, I remember him as he was, with his way of laughing and walking, taking me by the hand to the funfair to see the huge, frightening merry-go-rounds, and I forget about everything that ties him to his own social class. Each time I face this dilemma, I have to tear myself from the subjective point of view.

Naturally, I experience no joy in writing this book, seen as an undertaking in which I must remain close to the words and sentences I have heard. Occasionally I have resorted to italics. Not because I wish to point out a double meaning to the reader and so draw him into my confidence—irony, pathos and nostalgia are something I have always rejected. But simply because these particular words and sentences define the nature and the limits of the world where my father lived and which I too shared. It was a world in which language was the very expression of reality.

One day the little girl got back from school with a sore throat. Her temperature remained high; it was diphtheria. Like the other children in the Valley, she hadn't been vaccinated. My father was at the oil refinery when she died. When he got back home, his wailing could be heard from the far end of the street. He entered a state of shock which lasted for weeks, then went through a period of depression when he would just sit at the table and stare out of the window, refusing to speak. He would *beat himself* for the slightest thing. My mother would tell people, "She died when she was seven, just like a saint," drying her eyes with a cloth she produced from her apron pocket.

A photograph taken in the back yard, near the edge of the river. A white shirt with rolled-up sleeves, a pair of trousers, flannels most likely, sloping shoulders and slightly rounded arms. An expression of discontent on his face, maybe he wasn't quite ready for the photograph. He is forty years old. Nothing in the picture to account for the past suffering, or his hopes for the future. Just the obvious signs of age—the slight paunch, the receding hairline—and those, more discreet, of his social condition—his arms hanging stiffly at his sides and the washhouse and lavatory as a setting, hardly the choice of a middle-class person.

He wasn't called up in 1939, he was already too old. The oil refinery was burnt down by the Germans and so he took to the roads on his bicycle. She was six months' pregnant and had been offered a lift in someone's car. In Pont-Audemer he caught some shrapnel in his face and was treated at the only chemist that was open. The bombing continued. On the steps outside the basilica in Lisieux, he met up with his mother-in-law, accompanied by her daughters and their children. They had brought bags stuffed with their belongings. The steps and the esplanade were swarming with refugees. They thought they would be safe there. When the Germans entered the town, he returned to L—. The grocery store had been ransacked from top to bottom by those who had stayed behind. My mother came back and I was born the following month. In school, when we couldn't understand sums, they called us the "war children."

Up to the mid-fifties, this war epic would be recited in unison at Christmas dinners and confirmation receptions, with the inevitable chorus describing the fear, cold and hunger during the winter of 1942. *Despite everything one had to go on living.* Every week my father cycled thirty kilometres to an old warehouse which the local wholesalers no longer used. He brought the goods home on a cart hitched up to his bicycle. During the heavy bombing which hit that part of Normandy in 1944, he continued to go for fresh supplies, begging for extras for old people, large families and all those who couldn't afford to buy on the black market. In the Valley he was seen as a hero. He acted this way because he had to, not because he chose to. Looking back, he felt sure he had contributed something and had lived the war years to the full.

On Sundays they closed the business and went for a walk in the woods, where they picnicked on custard tarts made without eggs. He carried me on his shoulders, singing and whistling as he walked along. During air raids we would hide under the billiard table with the dog. When he thought back to that period, he had the feeling "it was fate." At the time of the Liberation he taught me to sing *La Marseillaise*, adding *"tas de cochons"* at the end to rhyme with *"sillons."* Like the other people around him, he was in a gay, lively mood. When we heard the sound of a plane, he took me by the hand and led me outside into the street. He told me to look at the bird in the sky: the war was over.

Heartened by the spirit of optimism that swept France in 1945, he decided to leave the Valley. I was often ill and the doctor wanted to send me to a sanatorium. They sold the business and moved back to Y—, where they believed the dry, windy climate—there were no streams or rivers—would be good for my health. We travelled in the front of the removal van and arrived in Y— at the height of the October fair. The town had been burnt down by the Germans and the booths and merry-go-rounds rose from amongst the debris. For three months they lived in a small two-room flat with mud floors and no electricity, which had been lent to them by one of the family. None of the businesses they could afford were for sale. My father got a job filling in the holes left by the shells. In the evening my mother would comment, holding the rail for dishcloths which one found on old-fashioned gas cookers, "How low can you get." He never replied. In the afternoon she would take me for a walk all round town. Only the centre of Y— had been bombed and the shops had been set up in private houses. Just one image, to illustrate the extent of the deprivations we endured: one day—night has already fallen—in a narrow window, the only patch of light in the street, pink, oval sweets sprinkled with white sparkle in their cellophane bags. They weren't for us, we didn't have any coupons.

They found a business in a rural area half-way between the station and the old people's home: a café-cum-grocery store which also supplied coal and firewood. As a child, my mother was sent there to do the shopping. It was a farmer's cottage with an extension in red brick at one end and came with a garden, a large courtyard and several outhouses used for storage. To get from the shop to the café, one walked through a tiny room with a staircase leading up to the attic and bedrooms. Although this became the kitchen, the customers continued to use it as a passageway. The goods that needed to be kept in a dry place—coffee, sugar— were stored on the stairs and around the bedroom walls. The ground floor afforded no privacy whatsoever. The lavatory was in the back yard. At last we were living *in the fresh air.*

My father's life as a worker stops here.

There were several cafés nearby but his was the only grocery store in the area. The town centre remained in ruins for a long time and the smart delicatessens of the pre-war period had temporarily been set up in yellow huts. Now there was nobody to *do them any harm.* (This expression, like so many others, is inseparably linked to my childhood. I have to concentrate to exorcise the suggestion of threat it carried in those days.) Unlike the working-class population in L——, the people from our neighbourhood were artisans, blue-collar workers employed by the gas board or by middle-sized factories, and old age pensioners belonging to the "lower-income bracket." The families here tended to keep to themselves. Stone-built houses separated by railings stood alongside low, single-storey tenements giving on to a shared courtyard. There were small vegetable gardens everywhere.

It was a café for regulars, habitual drinkers who dropped in before or after work and whose place was sacred: gangs from the building sites, as well as a few customers whose *position* meant they could have chosen a less proletarian establishment: a retired naval officer and an inspector from the national health service. In other words, *humble* people. The Sunday clientele was different, with whole families rolling in for an aperitif around eleven, lemonade for the children. In the afternoon it was the men from the old people's home who had been allowed out until six. They were a merry, noisy lot and enjoyed singing popular songs. Occasionally, when they'd had one too many, they had to sober up on a blanket in one of the outhouses before being fit to be sent back to the nuns. Going to their Sunday local was like visiting the family. My father was aware of the social role he played by offering a temple of freedom and rejoicing to those who, as he put it, "had not always been like that," although he couldn't exactly say why they had turned that way. Obviously, for those who had never set foot in the café, it was just a "boozer" where one drank oneself silly. The girls employed by the underwear factory next door would turn up after work to celebrate birthdays, weddings and departures. From the shop they bought packets of sponge fingers which they dipped into *vin mousseux*, bursting into peals of laughter, bent double over the café tables.

As I write, I try to steer a middle course between rehabilitating a lifestyle generally considered to be inferior, and denouncing the feelings of estrangement it brings with it. This was the way we lived and so of course we were happy although we realized the humiliating limitations of our class. (We knew full well that "it wasn't quite good enough at our place.") Consequently I would like to convey both the happiness and the alienation we felt. Instead, it seems that I am constantly wavering between the two.

Although he is approaching fifty, he is still in his prime, his head held perfectly straight and a worried expression on his face, as if he is afraid the photograph will come out wrong. He is wearing a suit—dark trousers and a light jacket—over a shirt and tie. The snapshot was taken on a Sunday. During the week he would have been wearing his overalls. Anyway one always took photos on Sundays because one had more time and was properly dressed. I am pictured beside him in a flounced dress, both arms outstretched, holding the handlebars of my very first bike, one foot touching the ground. He has one hand on his belt while the other is dangling at his side. In the background, the open door of the café, the flowers on the window sill and, just above, the plaque bearing the liquor licence. One always likes to be photographed with one's proudest possessions, in his case, the business, the bicycle, and later the Citroën 4CV. He is resting one hand on the roof of the car, causing his jacket to ride up around his shoulders. None of the photos shows him smiling.

Compared to his early youth, the shift work at the oil refinery and the rats in the Valley, it was plainly a life of happiness. We had everything that was *necessary*, in other words, we didn't go hungry—we bought meat from the butcher's four times a week—and the two rooms where we lived, the café and the kitchen, were properly heated. I had two sets of clothes, one for school days and one for Sundays. (When the former was worn out, the Sunday clothes would be *extended* to weekdays.)

I had *two* pinafores for class. *The child has everything she needs.* Nobody at the convent school could say I *wasn't as good* as the other girls. I had *just as many things* as the chemist's or the landowner's daughter: dolls, rubbers, pencil sharpeners, fur-lined winter shoes, not to mention my rosary and my Roman Catholic missal.

They were able to smarten up the place, getting rid of everything that looked old-fashioned, the beams, the fire-place, the wooden tables and the straight-backed chairs with their straw seats. With its flowered wallpaper, its shiny, newly painted bar and its table tops in fake marble, the café looked bright and clean. The wooden flooring in the bedrooms was covered with large, alternating squares of brown and yellow linoleum. For a long time their only source of frustration was the half-timbered façade, with its black and white stripes. Re-storing the outside of the building in roughcast was something they couldn't afford. One of my schoolmistresses walked by one day and said what a pretty house it was, a true Norman-dy cottage. My father thought she was saying that just to be polite. Those who admired the old things we had, the water pump in the yard and the rustic half-timbering, only wanted to prevent us from acquiring the new things they already pos-sessed, like running water and clean, whitewashed walls.

He took out a loan to buy the premises and the land. No one in the family had ever owned property before.

Although he was happy, he resented having to struggle for his livelihood. *I've only got one pair of hands. Too busy even to take a leak. Walking, that's how I get rid of my flu.* And so on. The daily chorus.

How can I describe a world in which everything had its price. There was the smell of freshly laundered linen on an October morning, and the latest tune heard on the radio running around in my head. Suddenly my dress gets caught on the handlebars of my bike and the fabric tears. It's the end of the world. The shouting. The day is ruined. The child just doesn't *think!*

Through necessity we came to treasure our possessions. My parents saw greed and envy in everything they heard, even when it came from their own daughter. When I told them: 'One of the girls went to see the châteaux of the Loire,' they would snap angrily, 'You can go later on in life. Be happy with what you've got.' A continual wanting, never satisfied.

They only really longed for things for the sake of it, because in actual fact they didn't know what was beautiful or what people were expected to admire. My father always followed the painter or the carpenter's advice when it came to choosing colours and shapes, *nothing fancy, just the standard thing.* He didn't even realize that some people collected objects one by one. Their bedroom wasn't decorated, just a few framed photographs, some table-mats made for Mother's Day and, on the mantelpiece, the large china bust of a child which the furniture man had given away as a free gift when they bought the corner settee.

His motto was, *"Better to be the head of a dog than the tail of a lion."*

He was always afraid of being ashamed or *out of place*. One day he got into a first-class compartment by mistake. The inspector made him pay the difference. Another embarrassing memory, a visit to the solicitor: he had to write "read and approved" but wasn't sure of the spelling. In the end he settled for "read and a proved." On the way back he suffered the pangs of humiliation, obsessed by his mistake. He had come close to disgracing himself.

Many of the comedies made around that time portrayed naïve country lads who didn't know how to behave in the city or in polite society (Bourvil-type roles). We would shriek with laughter at the things they said and the terrible gaffes they committed, the very ones we ourselves were afraid of making. I once read that when Bécassine* was serving her apprenticeship she was told to embroider a bird on the first bib and *ditto* on

* Fictional character invented by the French publisher Maurice Languereau for his children's weekly *La Semaine de Suzette*. Bécassine— from the French word *bécasse* meaning a ninny—is a naïve peasant girl from Brittany whose kind heart and easily abused incredulity lead her to commit one blunder after another. The series was illustrated by the cartoonist Jean-Pierre Pinochon and enjoyed tremendous popular success before and immediately after the First World War.

all the others. She spent the whole afternoon sewing *ditto* in satin-stitch. I wasn't sure that I wouldn't have done the same thing.

In front of people whom he considered to be important, his manner was shy and gauche and he never asked any questions. In short, he behaved intelligently. He realized we were inferior and refused to accept this, while at the same time doing everything he could to conceal the fact. We spent a whole evening wondering what on earth the headmistress had meant when she had said: "To play the part, your little girl will be dressed in *town clothes*." We were ashamed at not knowing what we would have known instinctively, had we not been what we were, in other words, inferior.

His obsession: *"What are people going to say?"* (the neighbours, the customers, the world at large).

His maxim, never to lay oneself open to criticism, was achieved by being polite, remaining neutral and keeping a tight rein on one's temper, so as not to do or say anything one might regret later. If one of the neighbours was digging up the garden vegetables, he never looked in his direction unless he was encouraged to do so by a smile, a nod or a friendly remark. He never visited anyone without being invited, not even somebody in hospital. He never asked questions which might betray envy or curiosity, so as not to give people a hold over us. The question "How much did you pay for it?" was taboo.

Now I often say "we" because I shared his way of thinking for a long time and I can't remember when I stopped doing so.

The local dialect was the only language my grandparents spoke.

There will always be people to appreciate the "picturesque charm" of *patois* and popular speech. Proust, for instance, took delight in pointing out the mistakes and the old-fashioned words used by Françoise. His concern, however, was purely aesthetic, because Françoise was not his mother but his maid, and because he knew these expressions were not natural to him.

My father saw *patois* as something old and ugly, a sign of inferiority. He was proud to have stopped using certain idioms. Even if his French wasn't perfect, at least it was French. During the fête in Y——, those who had the gift of the gab would dress up in traditional costume and perform sketches in Norman French while onlookers roared with laughter. The local paper had a regional column written in a lighthearted tone. When the doctor or some other *high-ranking* official peppered his speech with provincialisms—"she's as fit as a Malley bull on Sundays" instead of "she's bursting with health"—my father would repeat the sentence to my mother, relishing the thought that such respectable people still had something in common with us, some small "inadequacy." He was convinced that they had let it slip out inadvertently. He found it impossible to believe that speaking "properly" came naturally to some people. Whether a priest or a local GP, one had to make an effort to watch one's language, even if one lapsed into *patois* at home.

He was chatty with the customers and with us but in front of educated people he would remain quiet or would pause in mid-sentence, adding, "You know what I mean," with a vague gesture of his hand, willing the other person to finish the sentence for him. He always spoke carefully, terrified of using the wrong word, which would have been as bad as breaking wind.

On the other hand he hated high-falutin sentences and new expressions which "didn't mean anything." At one period everyone had taken to saying, "Surely not." He couldn't understand why people would use two words which meant exactly the opposite. Unlike my mother, who was anxious to pass for an educated woman and who tried out the idioms she had read or heard somewhere, with only a flicker of hesitation, he refused to use words that weren't from his world.

As a child, when I tried to express myself correctly, it was like walking down a dark tunnel.

One of my imaginary fears was about having a school-master

for a father, a man who forced me to speak properly all the time, articulating each word separately. One was supposed to speak with the whole of one's mouth.

Because the schoolmistress corrected me, I naturally wished to correct my father and tell him that expressions like "to dis-remember" and "somewhen" simply *didn't exist*. He flew into a terrible rage. On another occasion I burst out: "How do you expect me to speak properly if you keep on making mistakes?" I was crying. He felt miserable. Looking back, I realize now that anything to do with language was a source of resentment and distress, far more than the subject of money.

He was a cheerful man.

He would often joke with the customers who enjoyed a good laugh. Veiled references to sex. Scatological allusions. Irony was not his forte. On the radio he listened to quizzes and the programmes with *chansonniers*. He was always ready to take me to the circus, the fireworks or to see *silly* films. At the funfair we went on the ghost train and the big dipper, and visited the tent to see the fattest woman in the world and the Lilliputian.

He had never set foot in a museum. He would pause to admire a pretty garden, a cluster of trees in blossom or a beehive, and had an eye for fleshy girls. He liked towering buildings and huge, modern constructions, like the toll bridge at Tancarville.

He enjoyed circus music and going for drives in the country. In other words, if he could gaze at the fields and beech groves while listening to the Bouglione orchestra, he seemed happy. The emotion one feels on hearing a popular tune or admiring a pretty landscape was hardly a subject of conversation. When I first started going out with my middle-class school friends in Y—, they always wanted to know what I liked—jazz or classical music, Jacques Tati or René Clair. I soon realized that I had entered a new world.

One summer he took me to stay with the family for three days, down by the seaside. Out walking, he wore sandals over his bare feet, stopped to have a look at the German block-houses and sat at pavement cafés, ordering beer for himself and orangeade for me. He killed a chicken for my aunt, holding it between his legs and plunging a pair of scissors down its throat. The thick, greasy blood dripped on to the mud floor of the cellar. They didn't get up from lunch until the middle of the afternoon. They spent their time reminiscing about the war, the family, and passing round photographs over the empty cups. *"Ah, the hell with it, let's enjoy life while we can!"*

Maybe his true nature was just to take things easy after all. He invented things to do which kept him away from the business. Raising rabbits and chickens, building new outhouses or starting on a garage. The appearance of the courtyard would alter according to his whims; the lavatory and henhouse changed place three times. He felt a compulsive urge to demolish and rebuild.

My mother would say: "Well, what do you expect, he's a countryman."

He knew all the birds by their song and every evening he inspected the sky to see what the weather would be like: cold and dry if the horizon was red, windy and rainy if the moon was "water-deep," which meant wreathed in clouds. Every afternoon he would run off to his vegetable patch, which was always neat and tidy. Having an unkempt garden and neglecting one's vegetables was a sure sign of slovenliness, like drinking too much or being careless about one's appearance. It also meant that one had lost the notion of seasons—when certain varieties needed to be planted—and that one had given up worrying about what people thought. Occasionally notorious drunks would redeem themselves by cultivating a pretty garden between binges. When my father had failed to produce perfect leeks, or some other vegetable, he despaired. At the end of the day he would empty the night bucket into the last row he had dug up, furious if he discovered a pair of old stockings or some used biros I had chucked in during the day, because I couldn't be bothered to go downstairs.

When he ate, he insisted on using his Opinel clasp-knife. He cut up the bread into cubes which he stacked next to his plate; he skewered these with pieces of cheese and pork sausage and dipped them into the sauce. It grieved him to see me leave food on my plate. His own could have been put straight back into the cupboard. When the meal was over, he cleaned the knife on his overalls. If he had been eating herrings, he stuck it into the ground to get rid of the smell. Up to the late fifties, he drank soup in the morning. Later he changed for coffee with milk, with reluctance, as if he were giving in to some feminine delicacy. He drank it with a spoon, sipping it as if it were soup. At five o'clock he made his own tea—eggs, radishes, stewed apples—and was happy with a bowl of soup in the evening. Mayonnaise, cakes and heavy sauces made him feel sick.

He always slept in his shirt and his vest. He shaved three times a week in the mirror above the kitchen sink. He would undo the top buttons of his shirt and I could see the pale, white skin below his neck. Private bathrooms—seen as a sign of prosperity—were becoming more and more widespread after the war. My mother had a small washroom installed on the landing but he never used it and continued to wash downstairs in the kitchen.

Out in the courtyard, in winter, he spat and sneezed with relish.

Had it been considered acceptable, I could have given a description of him back at school, in an essay. One day, one of the girls, in her last year at primary school, gave a magnificent "atishoo" which sent her exercise book flying across the desk. The schoolmistress was writing on the blackboard. She turned round and exclaimed: "Really! Some people's manners!"

None of the middle-class people in Y— (white-collar workers, shopkeepers from the town centre) want to look as if they have "come up from the country." Being taken for a labourer means that one isn't educated and that one's general appearance, along with the way one speaks and dresses, is outdated. A popular anecdote at the time: a labourer who had gone into town to see his son sits down opposite the washing machine in the kitchen. He stares thoughtfully at the soapy water and the laundry going round and round. After a while he gets up, turns to his daughter-in-law and says with a shake of the head: "I don't know, it seems to me that television has still got a long way to go."

In Y—, however, one was less critical of the wealthy landowners who would turn up at the market in their brand new

Simca Vedette, to be replaced by a Citroën DS, and later by a Citroën CX. There was nothing worse than looking and behaving like a farmer when you weren't one.

He and my mother would invariably address each other in reproachful tones, even when they were showing concern. "Don't forget to take your muffler!" and "Why don't you sit down for a while?" sounded like insults. They would always be bickering over trifles: who had lost the supplier's invoice or who had left the light on in the cellar. Her voice rose above his because everything *got on her nerves*, a late delivery, her monthly period, the customers, or the dryer at the local hairdresser's, which was always too hot. Sometimes she would snap: "You weren't cut out to be a shopkeeper!" (which meant, you should have remained a worker). He responded to the insult by shedding his customary reserve: "*You slut!* I should have left you back where I found you!"

Every week they would exchange insults:

"A nobody, that's what you are!"

"And you're raving mad!"

"You're pathetic!"

"You stupid old bitch!"

And so on. It didn't mean anything.

At home, when we spoke to one another, it was always in a

querulous tone of voice. Only strangers were entitled to polite behaviour. The habit was so deep-rooted that my father—who applied himself to speaking properly in front of other people—would automatically revert to Norman French and to his broad accent and aggressive tone whenever he told me not to climb on to the heap of rubble in the yard. This ruined his efforts to create a good impression. He always used popular speech when he scolded me. Besides, if he had spoken properly, I would never have taken seriously his threats about slapping me.

For a long time courtesy between parents and children remained a mystery to me. Also, it took me years to "understand" the kindliness with which well-mannered people greet one. At first, I felt ashamed. After all, I didn't deserve such consideration. Sometimes I thought they had conceived a particular liking for me. Later I realized that their smiling faces and kind, earnest questions meant nothing more to them than eating with their mouth shut or blowing their noses discreetly.

Now it is imperative that I unravel these memories, all the more so since I have long suppressed them, believing them to be of no consequence. If they have survived, it is through sheer humiliation. I surrendered to the will of the world in which I live, where memories of a lowly existence are seen as a sign of bad taste.

In the evening, when I spread out my homework on the kitchen table, he would leaf through my books, especially the ones about history, geography and natural science. He liked to be tested on these subjects. One day he insisted that I gave him a dictation, to prove that he could spell properly. He never knew which form I was in. He would say, "She's with Miss So-and-so." My school—a religious establishment chosen by my mother—was seen by him as a terrifying world which dictated the whole of my behaviour, floating above me like the island of Laputa in *Gulliver's Travels*: "Honestly! If your schoolmistress could see you now!" or "I'll have a word with your teacher and she'll put you right!"

He always said *your* school and pronounced Moth-er Soo-peer-ior (which was how one addressed the headmistress) and con-vent school with deferential regard, taking care to separate each syllable. As if the normal pronunciation implied he was intimate with the closed world that these words evoked, a liberty he was not prepared to take. He refused to go to the school fête, even if I was in the play. This annoyed my mother, "*There's no reason why you shouldn't go*," to which he replied, "You know very well I never go in for *all that*."

Quite often, there was a serious, almost dramatic tone in his voice: "Listen carefully to what they tell you at school!" Afraid that my good marks—seen as some happy quirk of fate—would suddenly cease. Every time I did well in composition, and later in my exams, he saw it as an *achievement* and the hope that one day I might be *better than him*.

I wonder when this dream came to replace his own dream, which, he once confessed, was to run a smart café in town, one with passing trade, complete with terrace and a coffee machine behind the bar. Nothing came of it: insufficient funds, reluctance to start on something new and a defeatist attitude to life. *What do you expect?*

He was never to leave his small shopkeeper's world, irremediably split into two. On one side, there were the good customers, the ones who came to him, and on the other, the bad customers, the majority in fact, the ones who went shopping elsewhere, in the new part of town. The government was of course bracketed with the bad as he suspected them of wanting to ruin us by favouring *big business*. Even the good customers were divided into two groups. The good ones did all their shopping with us while the others snubbed us by dropping in for the odd pint of milk which they had forgotten to buy in town. And even then, the good ones weren't to be trusted: they were always afraid of being done and would walk out on us at the slightest opportunity. The whole world was locked in a conspiracy. There was hatred and servility, and the hatred he felt towards his own servility. Deep down inside he cherished the dream of every shopkeeper: to be the only one in town to sell his goods.

We walked one kilometre to get the bread because the baker next door didn't shop with us.

He voted for Poujade on principle, but without conviction; the man was too much of a braggart for his liking.

No one could say he was unhappy. There was the warm café, the music playing in the background and the stream of regular customers from seven in the morning to nine o'clock at night, prompting the ritual exchange of greetings: "Hello, mate, how are things then?"—"Oh not too bad I suppose." There were the conversations about the rain, people's health, the dead, unemployment or the bad drought that year. Statements of facts, variations on a theme. And then the last one for the road: "Cheers, squire"—"Cheers, be seeing you." Ashtrays were emptied, tables cleaned and chairs wiped.

If he had a free moment he would replace my mother in the shop. He didn't enjoy it. He preferred to spend his time in the café, or maybe not, maybe he just liked to potter around in the garden or knock away at the buildings in the back yard. The smell of privet blossom in late spring and the crisp, clear sounds of dogs barking and trains passing in November—a sure sign of cold weather: yes, he had everything that makes the powerful, the influential and the writers in newspapers say, "Ah, but they're happy after all."

Sundays meant a proper wash, a visit to church and, in the afternoon, a few games of dominoes or a drive round the country. On Mondays it was putting out the dustbin, on

Wednesdays dealing with the wine and spirits rep, on Thursdays buying the grocery supplies and so on. Twice in summer they would close the business for a whole day, to go and see friends—a railwayman and his family—and to make the pilgrimage to Lisieux. In the morning they visited the Carmelite chapel, the diorama and the basilica, ending up at their usual restaurant for lunch. In the afternoon they went to Les Buissonnets and Trouville-Deauville. He turned up his trouser legs and went for a paddle while my mother bunched up her skirts. They stopped going when it went out of fashion.

Sundays also meant having a good, decent meal at home.

From then on, his life was to remain unchanged. But anyway he felt that you can't be happier than you already are.

He'd had a nap that Sunday afternoon. I get a glimpse of him as he walks past the attic window. He is holding a book which he returns to the crate that the naval officer has left in storage. He chuckles as he catches sight of me in the courtyard. It's a dirty book.

A photograph of me on my own, standing in the courtyard, with the row of outhouses on my right, the old alongside the new. At the time I may not have been concerned with aesthetics but I certainly knew how to make the most of myself: a narrow skirt hugs hips flattered by a three-quarter profile, my shoulders are thrown back to emphasize my bust and a lock of hair is arranged on my forehead. I am smiling, so as to soften my features. I am sixteen years old. In the foreground one can see the shadow of my father, who took the picture.

I would spend all day in my room, learning my lessons, playing records and reading. I came down only for meals. We ate in silence. At home I never laughed. I indulged in "sarcasm." During this period I broke away from the things that were closest to me. I was slowly drifting into middle-class circles, where I gained admittance to teenage parties. All one had to do to get in was prove that one wasn't soppy—and that was so difficult. Now everything I liked seemed provincial, Luis Mariano, the romantic fiction by Marie-Anne Desmarets and Daniel Gray, lipstick, and the doll I had won at the funfair, resting on my pillow in her sequined dress. Even the ideas coming from my own background seemed ridiculous, people's preconceptions, for instance, "We'll always need the police," or "You're not a man till you do your national service." The whole world capsized.

I read "proper" literature and copied out verses and sentences which I thought expressed the state of my "soul" and the "elusive" quality of my life, like, "Happiness is a god who walks empty-handed" (Henri de Régnier).

My father became what was known as a humble man, a simple man or a good man. He no longer dared to tell me stories about his childhood. I stopped talking to him about school. Apart from Latin (as a boy he had served at mass), my lessons were incomprehensible to him but unlike my mother he didn't pretend to take an interest. He got cross when I criticized the curriculum or complained that I had too much work. He didn't like the words "break," "lines," or even "prep." He constantly feared—*or maybe hoped*—that I would never make it.

It annoyed him to see me studying all day and he blamed the books for my bad moods and the sullen expression on my face. The light under my door at night gave him cause to say that I was ruining my health. Study was the price one had to pay to get a decent job and avoid *ending up with a worker*. The fact that I actually enjoyed learning was suspicious to him. Missing out on life in the bloom of youth. Sometimes he seemed to think I was unhappy.

In front of the family and customers, he was embarrassed, almost ashamed by the fact that I still wasn't earning a living at the age of seventeen. All the other girls my age had jobs in offices or factories, or else worked in their parents' shop. He was afraid people would think me idle, afraid too he would pass as a braggart. He often said by way of an apology: "You know, we didn't force her, she had it in her." He used to say I was a good learner, never a good worker. One only worked with one's hands.

For him, school had nothing to do with ordinary life. Because he never washed the lettuce more than once, one often found slugs in the salad. He was scandalized when, after learning hygienics in the fourth form, I suggested that we change the water several times. On another occasion he was dumbfounded to hear me speak English with a hitchhiker who had been given a lift by one of the customers. The fact that I had learnt a foreign language at school, without ever visiting the country, was beyond his comprehension.

During this period he would occasionally fly into a terrible rage which twisted his features into a rictus of hate. My mother and I were very close at that time. It was all about monthly pains, beauty products and choosing the right bra. She took me shopping in the rue du Gros-Horloge in Rouen and then we went to the Périer tearooms, where we ate pastries with silver forks. She wanted to use the same expressions as me—"having a smooch," "she's the tops" and so on. We didn't need him.

At mealtimes the slightest thing would spark off an argument. I always thought I was right because he was incapable of holding a rational discussion. I criticized his table manners and the way he spoke. Obviously, I couldn't blame him for not being able to send me away on holiday but I felt I had the right to want him to improve his manners. Maybe he would have liked his daughter to be different.

One day he said: "Books and music are all right for you. I don't need them *to live*."

The rest of the time he led a quiet life. When I got back from school, he would be sitting in the kitchen, right next to the door that led into the café. He would be reading Paris-Normandie, his shoulders hunched, both arms resting on the newspaper which was spread out on the table. He would look up. "Ah here comes the lass."

"I'm starving!"

"There's nothing wrong with that. Take whatever you want."

At least he was happy to feed me. We talked about the same things we used to when I was a little girl. Nothing else.

I imagined that I had nothing else to learn from him. His words and ideas wouldn't be heard in the French and philosophy lecture halls, or in the other girls' drawing-rooms, where one sat on crimson plush sofas. In summer, through the open window of my room, I could hear the regular sound of his spade hammering the freshly-dug earth.

Maybe I am writing because we no longer had anything to say to each other.

When we had moved back to Y—, the town centre was in ruins. Now it offered small, cream-coloured blocks with new shops that stayed lit all night. At weekends the local youth would hang around the streets or watch television in the cafés. The women from our neighbourhood did their Sunday shopping at the big food stores in town. My father finally got his roughcast façade and his neon signs. Ironically, the café-owners with flair were going back to half-timbering, fake beams and old-fashioned oil lamps. The evenings were spent over the accounts. "They wouldn't come even if you gave the stuff away." Every time a new shop opened in Y —, my father went round on his bicycle to have a look.

They struggled along over the years, managing to achieve an acceptable standard of living. Our neighbourhood became working-class. In place of the executives who had left for modern flats with bathrooms, one found more and more people belonging to the lower-income group, large families and young working-class couples who had applied for a council flat. "You can pay me tomorrow, I'll be seeing you around." The old boys from the hospice had died and their successors weren't allowed to return drunk. There were no regulars now, just people who dropped in for a quick one and who kept to themselves, paying cash as they left. Now he felt he ran a respectable business.

He came to fetch me from the holiday camp where I had been working as a supervisor. My mother shouted halloo from a distance and then I saw them. My father walked with hunched shoulders, his head bent on account of the sun. His ears were pink, probably because he had just had his hair cut. On the pavement, in front of the cathedral, they stood bickering about the best way to get home. They looked like people who weren't used to going out. In the car I noticed yellow stains at his temples, near his eyes. For the first time I had spent two months away from home, in a young, carefree world. My father was an old, worried man. I felt I no longer had the right to go to university.

He started to feel uncomfortable after meals, something vague and indefinite. He took milk of magnesia, afraid to call the doctor. He finally had an X-ray and the specialist in Rouen diagnosed a stomach polyp which needed to be removed immediately. My mother complained that he was always fussing over his health. Also, he felt guilty because he was costing them money. (In those days, tradesmen didn't benefit from the health service.) He would say: "Just my luck."

After the operation he remained in hospital for as little time as was permitted and began his slow recovery at home. His strength had left him. He could no longer lift crates or spend several hours gardening, otherwise he risked pulling a muscle. I remember the familiar scene of my mother rushing from the cellar to the shop or carrying the delivery boxes and the bags of potatoes, doing both their jobs. He lost his pride at the age of fifty-two. "I'm useless now." He was speaking to my mother. This may have meant several things.

Yet he was determined to get the better of it and start a new life for himself. He grew fond of his little comforts. He began to worry about his health. Food became something formidable which was either good or evil depending on whether it agreed with him or was shown the door. He sniffed a slice of beef or a fillet of fish before tossing it into the pan. He felt quite sick at the sight of my yoghurts. He discussed his diet in the café and at family gatherings, exchanging comments on homemade broth, powdered soup and so on. All the people around us who were approaching sixty held similar conversations.

He satisfied his craving for food: a pork sausage or a paper cone filled with shrimps. The glimpse of happiness they promised vanished after the first few mouthfuls. At the same time he pretended he wanted nothing and kept saying, "Just give me *half* a slice of ham," or "I'll have *half* a glass." He developed idiosyncracies, such as splitting open his *Gauloises*, throwing away the paper—which he said had a bad taste—and carefully rolling himself new cigarettes with *Zig-Zag*.

On Sundays, so as not to become *set in their ways*, they would go for a drive along the banks of the Seine and revisit the piers where he used to work, in Dieppe and Fécamp. His hands

would hang at his sides—fingers touching, palms facing out-
wards—or else they would be clasped behind his back. When he
walked he never knew what to do with his hands. In the evening
he would get back home exhausted. "Sunday's more tiring than
the other days of the week."

There were politics too, with the overriding question of
how's it all going to end (the Algerian war, the coup of the gener-
als, the acts of terrorism of the OAS) and his assumed intimacy
with the *great Charles*.

I entered the teachers' training college in Rouen to become a
primary schoolmistress. I was fed—overfed one could say—and
my laundry was done for me. There was even an odd-job man
to mend people's shoes. Free of charge. My father seemed to re-
spect this system, in which everything was subsidized. The State
was offering me a place in society from the start. He was at a
loss to understand why I left college before the end of the year.
He couldn't see why I had given up a haven of security—where
I was being fattened up like a goose—simply because I wanted
to be free.

I spent a long time in London. When I was away from
home, I was certain of his affection for me, which I saw as
something abstract. I was beginning to live my own life.
My mother kept me informed about what was going on in
the neighbourhood. It's turned quite cold down here I hope
it's not going to last. Sunday we went to see our friends in
Granville. Old Mrs So-and-so died she wasn't that old only

sixty. She never joked about anything in her letters, it was bad enough finding the right words and expressions. She hadn't learnt to write the way she spoke, that would have proved even more difficult. My father signed the letter. I replied in the same neutral tone. Any attempt at style would have been taken as a snub.

I came back home, then left again. I was studying literature at Rouen University. They argued less, just the usual bickering, out of habit: "I don't know what you do, hanging around at the church all day," or "We're out of orangeade again and we know who's to blame!" Although he still had plans to do up the place, he wasn't aware of the momentous changes that were needed to attract a new clientele. He made do with his own customers, the ones who were put off by the pristine stores in the new part of town, and by the snooty salesgirls who *looked one up and down*. He had lost all his drive. He had accepted the fact that his business was merely a means of survival which would disappear when he died.

He decided to *enjoy life*. He got up later, after my mother, did some light work in the café and the garden, read the newspaper from cover to cover and held long conversations with everybody. He would allude to death in the form of proverbs, *we all know what's waiting for us*. Every time I came home, my mother would say: "Look at your father! He's in clover!"

It is late summer—September. He catches wasps off the windowpanes with his handkerchief and throws them on to the burner of the coal stove, already lit despite the time of year. They die twisting and turning while their bodies are slowly consumed.

He was neither worried nor excited to see me lead such a strange, surreal existence. He had come to terms with the fact that I was still learning at the age of twenty or more. "She's studying to become a teacher," he would tell customers. They never asked which subject, it was the title that mattered and anyway he could never remember. "Modern languages" didn't ring a bell for him like mathematics or Spanish might have done. He was afraid that people would think me privileged and that they would be seen as rich parents who had pushed me towards university. On the other hand he never admitted that I had been given a grant. People would say that they were darned lucky to have the State pay me to do nothing. He felt that he was continually exposed to the envy and jealousy of others. Maybe this was the most distinctive sign of his social condition. Sometimes I came in on a Sunday morning, having been out all night, and slept until the following evening. They never said a word. They even seemed to approve of my behaviour as it implied that I was normal after all—every girl's entitled to a bit of *good, clean fun*. It is possible too that they had romanticized notions of the intellectual, middle-class world I was frequenting, a world unknown to them.

If a factory girl was pregnant when she got married, the whole neighbourhood knew.

During the summer holidays I would invite a couple of friends from college to come and stay in Y—. *Unprejudiced* girls, who claimed that the main thing was to "have one's heart in the right place." To avoid any condescending remarks about my family, I had warned them: "I must tell you, it's very *basic* back at my place." My father was glad to welcome such well-educated young ladies. He took a keen interest in everything they did and spoke to them at great length, keeping the conversation going out of politeness. Planning meals was always a problem. "Does *mademoiselle* Geneviève eat tomatoes?" He went out of his way to please them. When I was a guest in their house, they didn't let my visit upset their routine. I was allowed to share their lifestyle and step into their world which, unlike mine, had nothing to hide, and which was open to me because I had forgotten the ways, the ideas and the tastes of my own background. In middle-class circles, having one's daughter's friends to stay is commonplace. My father treated these visits as a special occasion because he wanted to honour my friends and show them that he had manners. Instead he only managed to show he was inferior, a fact which they instinctively acknowledged by saying, for instance, "*How's it going*, sir?"

One day he said to me proudly: "I have never given you cause for shame."

One year, at the end of summer, I *brought home* a political science student to whom I was committed. This solemn ritual—which sanctions the right to enter a new family—was no longer observed in modern, middle-class households, where boyfriends came and went freely. To receive the young man, he put on a tie and changed his overalls for a pair of Sunday flannels. He was overjoyed because he believed that he would be able to treat my future husband as his own son and that the two of them would establish a male bond that would transcend their social differences. He showed him the garden and the garage that he had built with his own hands. He made this offering in the hope that his merits would be acknowledged by the man who loved his daughter. All they asked from the boy was that he had *good manners*. It was the quality they admired most because they saw it as a tremendous achievement. They didn't try to find out whether he was hardworking or whether he drank, as they would have in the case of a factory hand. They were convinced that being well read and well mannered were marks of an inner excellence that was natural in such people.

It was something they had been expecting for years maybe, a load off their mind. Now they knew I wouldn't end up with any *Tom, Dick or Harry*, or become a *social outcast*. He wanted his savings to go towards helping the young married couple. He hoped that this act of supreme generosity would iron out the social and cultural differences which separated him from his son-in-law. "There's not much your mother and I need now."

At the wedding reception, in a restaurant overlooking the Seine, he is sitting with his head held straight, both hands resting on a napkin in his lap. He is smiling gently, at no one in particular, as bored people often do when they are waiting for the next course. His smile also means that everything here today is perfect. He is wearing a blue pinstriped suit, specially made to measure, and a white shirt with, for the first time, a pair of cufflinks. The image is frozen in my memory. I had glanced in his direction while I was laughing with my guests, certain that he wouldn't be enjoying himself.

After that he only saw us every now and then.

We lived in a tourist resort in the Alps where my husband had been offered an executive position. We covered the walls with hessian, served whisky as an aperitif and listened to sixteenth-century music on the radio. A polite word or two to the *concierge*. My mother wrote saying: "Why not come and stay for a few days, it'd be a nice break," afraid to ask us over just to see them. I went alone, concealing the real reasons for their son-in-law's absence. My husband and I never discussed these reasons, I simply took them for granted. What could a man brought up in middle-class circles—where people got degrees and cultivated the art of irony—possibly have to say to *honest, hard-working people* like my parents? Although he acknowledged their kindness, in his eyes it would never replace a lively, witty conversation, sadly lacking in their case. In his family, for instance, if someone broke a glass, one would immediately cry out: "Touch it not, for it is broken!" (a quote from Sully Prudhomme's poem *Le Vase Brisé*).

It was always she who came to meet me from the Paris train. She waited for me by the barrier and insisted on taking my suitcase, "It's too heavy for you, you're not used to carrying things." In the shop there would probably be a couple of customers whom he stopped serving while he kissed me in his usual brusque manner. I sat down in the kitchen while they remained standing, she by the stairs, he silhouetted in the doorway that led through to the café. At that time of day the sun played upon the tables and the glasses on the counter; sometimes a customer listening to us was caught in the beam of sunlight. Away from home, I had stripped my parents of their speech and mannerisms, turning them into magnificent people. Now I was hearing their real voices again—loud and booming—and their broad Norman pronunciation, saying "*a*" in place of "*elle*." I realized they had always been like this, without the "decorum" and the language which I now considered to be normal. I felt torn between two identities.

I hand him the present I have brought with me. He unwraps it eagerly. It's a bottle of aftershave. There are embarrassed laughs, "What's it for?" Then he adds: "I'll smell like a tart now!" All the same he promises to use it. The typical scene of a badly chosen present. I feel like crying, "Won't he ever change?" as in the old days.

We talked about the people from our neighbourhood who had got married, died or left town. I described the flat, the Louis-Philippe writing desk, the hi-fi system and the red velvet armchairs. He soon lost interest. He had brought me up to enjoy the luxuries he himself had been denied, therefore he was happy, but the antique dresser and the Dunlopillo mattress meant nothing more to him than the signs of social success. He often cut me short by saying, "You're quite right to make the most of it."

I never stayed long enough. He gave me a bottle of Cognac for my husband. "Not to worry, we'll see him next time around." He was proud not to give anything away, keeping his feelings strictly under his hat.

The first supermarket opened in Y——, attracting a working-class clientele from all parts of town. At last one could do one's shopping without having to ask for everything. Yet one still troubled the local grocer for a bottle of unpasteurized milk, the jelly babies one bought on the way to school or the odd pound of coffee one had forgotten to get in town. He started thinking about selling the business. They could move into the adjoining house which they must have bought at the same time as the shop: a two-roomed flat with a kitchen and cellar. He would salvage some tins and a few good bottles of wine. He would keep hens for fresh eggs. They could come and see us in the Haute-Savoie. He already had the satisfaction of being on the health service at the age of sixty-five. When he got back from the chemist, he loved to settle at the table and arrange the stickers on his reimbursement sheet.

He enjoyed life more and more.

Several months have passed since I started this narrative last November. It has taken me a long time because I find it is far more difficult to dig up forgotten memories than it is to invent them. One's memory resists. I could not rely on personal reminiscence: the squeaky door-bell of an old grocer's shop and the smell of overripe melons would lead me to picture only myself and my summer holidays in Y—. The colour of the sky and the poplar trees reflected in the river Oise could teach me nothing. It was in other people that I searched for the figure of my father, in the way they would call their children, sit down and look bored in waiting rooms and wave goodbye on station platforms. Anonymous figures glimpsed on a street corner or on a crowded bus—unwittingly bearing the stamp of success or failure—brought back to me the reality of his condition.

Spring didn't come. I felt as though I had been locked in the same weather since November; it remained wet and mild even in the dead of winter. I hadn't been thinking about the end of my book. Now I know that the time is drawing near. The hot weather set in at the beginning of June. By sniffing the air one could tell it was going to be a nice day.

Soon I shall have nothing more to write. I would like to put off writing the last pages and always have them ahead of me. Yet it is already too late to go back on what has been said, to alter or to add details, or even to wonder what happiness meant for him. As usual I shall take an early morning train and I shan't get there until nightfall. This time I am bringing their two-and-half-year-old grandson to see them.

My mother was waiting for me at the barrier. She had

slipped the jacket of her two-piece suit over her shopkeeper's coat and had knotted a scarf around her head—she stopped dying her hair when I got married. The child, dumb with exhaustion and confused by such a long journey, let itself be kissed and led away by the hand. It wasn't quite so hot now. My mother still had her brisk, characteristic way of walking. Suddenly she slowed down, shouting gaily: "We mustn't forget his little legs, poor dear." My father was waiting for us in the kitchen. He didn't seem to have aged. My mother pointed out that he'd had his hair cut the day before in honour of his grandson. It was a muddled scene, with the two of them shouting, firing questions at the child without even waiting for answers and criticizing each other for exhausting the poor little fellow. But oh, they were so happy. They tried to work out which side of the family he took after. My mother showed him the jars of sweets. My father led him outside to see the strawberries, then the ducks and rabbits. They took him over completely and decided everything he should do, as if I were still a little girl incapable of looking after a child. They were skeptical about my notion of education: having an afternoon nap, cutting out sweets and so on. The four of us ate at the table by the window, with the child sitting in my lap. It was a magical evening, blissfully quiet, suggestive of redemption.

My old bedroom was still warm from the heat of the day. A small bed had been set up next to mine for the little one. After trying to read, I couldn't get to sleep for two hours. As soon as

I plugged in the bedside lamp, the wire blackened, sparks flew and the bulb went out. The lamp was in the shape of a ball resting on a marble base, with a brass rabbit sitting upright, its front paws sticking out at its sides. I had once thought it very beautiful. It must have been broken for ages. They never got anything mended at home, they didn't care.

Now, it's another moment in time.

I woke up late. My mother was speaking softly to my father in the next room. Later she told me he had been sick in the early hours before he'd even had time to reach the bucket. She assumed it was indigestion, caused by the chicken leftovers we'd had for lunch the previous day. He was anxious to know whether she'd cleaned the floor and complained about pains in his chest. His voice sounded different. When the little one went up to him, he paid him no attention and remained motionless, lying flat on his back.

The doctor went straight upstairs to see him. My mother was serving in the shop, but she joined him soon afterwards and the two of them came down together. As he reached the foot of the stairs, the doctor whispered that he ought to be taken to the hospital in Rouen. My mother broke down. From the very start she would say to me, "He insists on eating things that don't agree with him," and when she brought him his mineral water she would tell him, "You know perfectly well you've got a funny stomach." She kept twisting the clean napkin which the GP had used for his auscultation. She didn't seem to understand and couldn't accept the fact that my father's illness—which we had dismissed as indigestion—was really serious. The doctor suggested that we wait until that evening to make up our minds, after all it might only be the effect of the heat.

I went out to buy the medicine. The sky was grey and overcast. The chemist recognized me. There was hardly any more traffic in the streets now than on my previous visit the year before. Because everything here was just like it used to be when I was a child, I couldn't possibly imagine that my father was seriously ill. I bought some vegetables to make a stew. Some of the customers asked after the boss, surprised that he still wasn't up on such a fine day. They gave simple reasons for his indisposition, which they backed up with their own experience: "Yesterday it was at least 40° in the back garden. If I'd stayed out like him, I'd have fainted," or "This heat really gets one down, I couldn't eat a thing yesterday." Like my mother, they seemed to think that my father had fallen ill because he had challenged nature by behaving irresponsibly. He had got what he deserved but shouldn't do it again.

When it was time for his afternoon nap, the child walked past the bed and said: "Mummy, why is the gentleman sleeping?"

My mother would nip upstairs between customers. Every time the bell rang, I shouted out to her like I used to, so that she could come down and serve in the shop. Although he drank only water, his condition remained stable. When the doctor came round in the evening, he didn't mention the hospital again.

The next day, whenever my mother or myself asked him how he felt, he would snort angrily or complain that he hadn't eaten for two days. The doctor hadn't made a single joke about my father's health, as he usually did: "Not to worry, he's just farted backwards." Every time I watched him walk downstairs, I longed for him to come out with some pleasantry or other. That evening my mother said to me, lowering her gaze: "I don't know what's to come of all this." It was the first time she had acknowledged the fact that my father might die. For the past two days we had shared our meals and taken care of the child without mentioning his illness. I replied: "Well, we'll see." When I was about eighteen, she would sometimes snap: "If anything ever happens to you . . . you know what's left for you to do." It wasn't necessary to be more specific, we both knew exactly what she meant without her actually having to say the words: getting pregnant.

On Friday night my father's breathing became deep and laboured. Then we heard a loud, continual bubbling sound which was distinct from his breathing. It was horrible because we couldn't tell whether it was coming from his lungs or his stomach, as if the whole of his inner body communicated. The doctor gave him a shot to sedate him. He calmed down. In the afternoon I put some clean linen away in the cupboard. Out of curiosity I took a piece of pink ticking and held it against the edge of the bed. He propped himself up and watched me, telling me in his new voice: "It's to put on your mattress. Your mother's already done this one." He pulled on the blanket to show me his own mattress. It was the first time he had shown an interest in anything around him since he'd had his attack. At the time I thought this meant there was still hope. He spoke the words to prove that he wasn't ill, yet it was precisely because he was drifting away from this world that he was making such a desperate effort to cling to it.

After that he didn't speak to me again. He was perfectly lucid, turning over for his injection when he saw the nurse enter the room and answering my mother's questions with a yes or no: was he in pain or did he want anything to drink? Every so often he would decide to protest, "If only I could have something to eat," as if merely eating would cure him, a cure denied by some unknown authority. He couldn't remember how many days he had gone without food. My mother kept saying: "A bit of dieting's never harmed anyone." The child was playing in the garden. I kept an eye on him while I tried to read *Les Mandarins* by Simone de Beauvoir. It was a long book and I couldn't get into it. I knew that when I reached a certain page, my father would no longer be alive. The customers were still asking after him. They wanted to know exactly what the problem was, sun-stroke or a heart attack. They were dumbfounded by my mother's vague replies as they felt we were hiding something from them. For us, the name was no longer important.

On Sunday morning I was woken by a melodious mumbling, interrupted by pauses. The last rites of the Catholic Church, the most obscene ceremony of all. I buried my head in the pillow. My mother must have got up at the crack of dawn to catch the archpriest when he came out of his first service. Later that day I went upstairs to see him when my mother was serving the customers. I found him sitting on the edge of the bed, his head bent forward, staring desperately at the chair by his bed. He was holding an empty glass at the end of his outstretched arm. His hand was trembling violently. At first I didn't realize that he wanted to set the glass down on the chair. For several interminable seconds I watched his hand and the expression of despair on his face. Then I took the glass from him and put him back to bed, arranging his legs on top of the covers. I thought to myself: "I can do that," or "I must be a big girl now to be able to do that." Then I nerved myself to look at him properly. His face bore only a faint resemblance to the one I had known in the past. Around the dental plate, which he had insisted on keeping in, his lips had curled up, exposing his gums. He had become one of the ageing, bedridden men of the old people's home where we were taken by the headmistress of our convent school to bawl out Christmas carols. And yet it seemed to me that, even in this condition, he could have continued to live for some time.

At half-past twelve I put the child to bed. He wasn't sleepy and kept jumping up and down on his mattress. My father's breathing was laboured, his eyes wide open. My mother closed the shop and the café around one o'clock as she did every Sunday. Then she went back upstairs. My uncle and aunt arrived while I was doing the washing up. After seeing my father, they settled in the kitchen. I gave them some coffee. I heard my mother's footsteps cross the floorboards above and start to come downstairs. Despite her slow, deliberate pace, I thought she was coming down for her coffee. When she reached the bend in the staircase, she said softly: "It's all over."

The business has closed down. Now it's a private house with Terylene curtains hanging in what used to be the shop windows. It stopped being a business when my mother moved out. She now lives in a flat near the town centre. She ordered a beautiful marble memorial for my father's tomb. A— D— 1899–1967. Something simple, requiring no maintenance.

Now I have finished taking possession of the legacy with which I had to part when I entered the educated, bourgeois world.

One Sunday after church, when I was twelve years old, my father and I walked up the sweeping staircase inside the town hall. We were looking for the public library. I was terribly excited, we'd never been there before. We couldn't hear anything on the other side of the door. All the same my father pushed it open. It was completely quiet in the room, quieter even than in church. The floorboards creaked and there was a strange, musty smell in the air. Perched behind a high desk barring access to the shelves, two men watched us approach. My father let me say: "We'd like to borrow some books." One of them immediately asked: "What books do you want?" At home it hadn't occurred to us that we had to prepare a list and reel off titles as easily as if they had been brands of biscuits. They chose the books for us: Colomba for me and a light novel by Maupassant for my father. We never went back to the library. My mother must have returned the books, maybe when they were overdue.

He would take me to school on his bicycle, carrying me from one shore to the other, in fair or bad weather.

His greatest satisfaction, possibly even the *raison d'être* of his existence, was the fact that I belonged to the world which had scorned him.

He liked to sing: *For rolling in the dew makes the milkmaids so fair.*

I remember the title of a book which was *L'Expérience des Limites*. I was so disappointed when I started reading it, it was only about metaphysics and literature.

While I was writing this book I was also marking papers and sending out model essays because that's what I'm paid to do. That type of intellectual exercise aroused the same feelings in me as notion of *luxury*. Both were unreal and both made me want to cry.

In October last year, while I was queuing at the checkout with my trolley, I recognized one of my former students. Or rather I remembered that the cashier had been my student five or six years earlier. I couldn't recall her name or which class she'd been in. When it was my turn, just to say something, I asked her: "How are you doing? Do you like it here?" She replied, "Fine, yes, yes." After she had registered the drinks and tinned food, she said in an embarrassed voice: "It didn't work out at the technical school." She seemed to think that I still remembered her history. But I had forgotten why she had been sent to a technical college and which stream they had put her in. I said goodbye. She was already

on to the next customer, moving the stuff along with her left
hand while the right jabbed mechanically at the cash register.

November 1982–June 1983

Born in 1940, ANNIE ERNAUX grew up in Normandy. From 1977 to 2000, she was a professor at the Centre National d'Enseignement par Correspondance. She is the author of *Passion simple*, her first bestseller in France, and of many other novels. Her recent books include *Les années*, *L'écriture comme un couteau*, and the collection of her works, *Écrire la vie*. Many of her books have been published in the US, including *The Possession* and *A Woman's Story*, a *New York Times* Notable Book. *A Man's Place* was also a *New York Times* Notable Book and was a finalist for the *Los Angeles Times* Book Prize.

TANYA LESLIE has translated seven novels by Annie Ernaux. She lives in Paris where she has worked as a translator and editor for over twenty years and has contributed to the Paris-based literary journal *Frank*.

National Book Award finalist FRANCINE PROSE'S most recent work of fiction is *My New American Life*. Her other books include *Blue Angel, Anne Frank: The Book, The Life, The Afterlife*, and *Reading Like A Writer: A Guide for People Who Love Books and for Those Who Want to Write Them*. She is a Distinguished Visiting Writer at Bard College.